#1 blazing courage

ANIMAL RESCUES

#1 Blazing Courage

KELLY MILNER HALLS

darbycreek
MINNEAPOLIS

Darby Creek
A division of Lerner Publishing Group, Inc.
241 First Avenue North
Minneapolis, MN 55401 USA

For reading levels and more information, look up this title at www.lernerbooks.com.

Additional images: © iStockphoto.com/benz190 (grunge texture); © iStockphoto.com/Piotr Krześlak (paper texture).

Main body text set in Janson Text LT Std 12/17.5.
Typeface provided by Adobe Systems.

Library of Congress Cataloging-in-Publication Data

The Cataloging-in-Publication Data for *#1 Blazing Courage* is on file at the Library of Congress.
ISBN 978-1-4677-7219-8 (lib. bdg.)
ISBN 978-1-4677-9399-5 (pbk.)
ISBN 978-1-4677-8830-4 (EB pdf)

Manufactured in the United States of America
1 – BP – 7/15/15

To my father, Gene Milner,
who helped make my horse dreams come true.

CHAPTER ONE
The Auction

"Wait!" I yell. Jack Manley, my stable manager, is walking so fast I can hardly see him through the dust. hundreds of hooves can do that—raise a sandstorm in a stadium—especially when every hoof is up for auction.

"Keep up, Annie!" he bellows in his gruff, cowboy voice. "Do you want that mare or not?"

It's hard to believe the day has finally come. After a lifetime of collecting Breyer horses and Kathleen Duey novels, after thirteen months of cleaning tack and shoveling manure, I am about to buy a horse—as much horse as my two hundred and six dollars of savings can get me. More horse than I've ever had before.

The United States government takes care of miles and miles of open wilderness that is home to wild horses. When the herds get too big, they round a few up and sell them to the highest bidders. Jack had been studying the Colorado round-up horses for days to pick the right one for me.

"My choice is an Appaloosa," he says over his shoulder, "sixteen hands of spotted awesome. We should be able to get her for a song, if you get the lead out of your boots."

Jack's stride is so much longer than mine that I have to jog not to get left behind. He's fast for an old guy, and tall, but it's hard to tell. Fifty years of rodeo takes a toll. Break enough bones and you wind up crooked. I top out at five feet. I'm short enough to be a jockey, but too heavy; *pleasingly plump*, I overheard someone whisper once. So what? Horses don't care what you look like.

Hundreds of people fill the arena seats, most holding bidders' numbers. Our number is 1206—my birthday. Jack says that's a good sign. Only a hundred horses fill the red pipe corrals on the far end of the dirt arena floor. Some of the animals seem calm. Others, not so much. Jack explains the calm horses will go for more money, because they've been green broken.

"They've been sweet-talked," Jack says with a wink. "They don't think you're going to eat them, and they're rider ready." Then his smile disappears.

"What?" I say.

"She's here," Jack replies. "The Butcher."

Most of the people have turned out to buy riding horses cheap. Everyone from dude ranchers who give tourists a thrill to top trainers—all shopping for equestrian bargains. The best horses will go to them, but what about the rest?

"She'll buy a bunch of them," Jack growls. "She'll ship them to China, and they'll come back as dog food."

I feel sick to my stomach, and I can't help staring. She doesn't look evil. Boots to hat to braided gray hair, she looks ordinary. She glances our way and whispers to the man sitting next to her. He tips his black ball cap, and they laugh. I wonder, what could be funny about that job?

Jack nudges me. "Forget her. It's starting."

The auctioneer steps to the microphone. Auction workers lead horses, one at a time, to video cameras, and instantly they appear on the stadium Jumbotrons. People oooh and ahhh at each new horse. My heart beats like the wings of a dragonfly.

We wait for the Appaloosa Jack scouted, but I worry. A Paint mare built like a Quarter Horse goes for two hundred. A Palomino colt sells for two twenty five. A string of twenty-two horses sell for more than I have in my pocket, and the Appaloosa is still eight horses down the line.

I tug on Jack's sleeve to ask if he's worried too when a wave of laughter distracts me. A little four-year-old Buckskin slips out of her halter and gallops away from the handler. He chases after her, yelling, "Whoa!" The cameraman runs behind them. He's trying to get a shot for the video screen, but he gets too close. The horse bucks and kicks her back hooves inches from his face. He falls back into the dirt as she canters away, victorious. I smile.

Jack leans back and tips his hat over his eyes, our bidding paddle on his lap. Wrangling this little cyclone could take a while, so he settles in for a catnap. But the Butcher isn't resting. Her eyes follow the mud-caked Buckskin. Her number is in the air as she bids $30 for the stubborn little horse.

"I hear forty," says the auctioneer. A second person—I don't see who—bids, just before the handler corners the horse and slips the halter back on her head. She bites him hard on the shoulder, then pulls back against the lead rope. In a panic, she rears up on her hind legs, fighting for her freedom. The Butcher smiles and raises her paddle.

Silence fills the arena, as the auctioneer says, "Fifty? Do I hear fifty dollars? Anyone?"

All eyes move to the next horse in line as the auctioneer raises his gavel to make it final—all eyes but mine. "Forty-five, once," he calls. By the time he says, "Forty-five, twice," I am on my feet, but I don't know what to do to stop it. I lean forward, my eyes locked on the Butcher, willing her to disappear somehow.

"Fifty!" cries the auctioneer. I don't see the paddle but relief washes over me, and I continue my death stare at the Butcher. *Let her go*, I think. *Let her go.*

The auctioneer looks at the Butcher, asking if she wants to raise her bid, but she shakes her head no. I feel relief for the first time since the bidding began. "Take that," I say under my breath. She sinks back in her chair, waiting for her next victim.

The auctioneer slams the wooden gavel and shouts, "SOLD! A crazy little Mustang to bidder 1-2-0-6. Congratulations, Jack!"

I spin like a top to face Jack. He's smiling like a jack-o-lantern. "Only fourteen hands," he says, "good thing you're small." We walk to the truck to prepare the trailer, and he continues. "Guess what? You can buy a cheap saddle now, too."

CHAPTER TWO
Going Home

Jack lets me lead the little mare from the arena to the horse trailer, but he stays close. "She's unpredictable," he says. "Keep your wits about you."

Her nostrils flare as we move outside. The fresh air comforts her. But getting her into the trailer could be trouble. A sign of things to come, Jack says, but I don't care. All I can do is stroke her black mane, her pink muzzle. I trace my fingers across the white patch on her face.

It makes her eye seem electric brown. My own horse. I almost can't believe it.

"She's bald faced," Jack says. "That's what it's called when most of a horse's face is white, but its body isn't." Ugly name for a beautiful mark, I think. He takes the lead rope from me and tells me to step inside the front section of the trailer. He unwinds the lead rope to make it longer and hands me the lose end.

"Remember," he says. "Unpredictable."

I watch her, holding the lead in one hand, a bag of apple slices in the other. I see fear in her eyes, but not panic. She watches me, but she hasn't yet taken a step inside the trailer. Forcing her could be suicide. As scared as she is, if anyone shoved from behind, she'd kick their teeth out. Worse, she could take a step in, rear up, and break her neck on the roof of the trailer.

"Slow and easy," Jack says as he walks to the back of the trailer. He hands one end of a long, thick rope to an auction aid and holds the other end himself. Jack moves to the right side of the trailer, the auction man moves to the left, and slowly they take up the slack until the rope is resting on the Buckskin's haunches. As they pull tighter, the Buckskin feels pressure on her hips that urges her to move forward. But she is not happy about it, and her ears go back to prove it.

"Start to pull her lead rope," Jack says, trying not to yell. "And try to keep her calm."

"Hey little girl," I whisper as I gather up the slack. "We're going to be good friends, you and I." Her tan ears move forward, and so does her body. She doesn't know what I'm saying, but she studies the tone of my voice.

"Come on, girl. I already love you. Can't you love me a little?" I offer her a slice of apple.

She makes a soft, reassuring sound, a nicker deep inside her throat—like the purr of an oversized, untamed kitten. I wonder how long it's been since she's eaten. She breathes deeply, then slowly moves toward me, all the way into the trailer. As she takes the treat from the palm of my hand, I smile.

"You like that?" I ask, as I pull another piece from the bag. She takes it, too. "I'm glad," I say. "You'll like me, too. You'll see." Her muscles tense as Jack slams the back trailer door and locks the latch. She's alert and unsure but still taking bits of apple. For now, she's decided to stay calm.

"Time to head home," Jack says, petting the Mustang's forelock. I step out of the trailer cabin and head for the passenger side of his old truck. All I can do is smile as I put on the seatbelt.

"Look at you," Jack says, snickering, "All that homeschooled smart girl melted away to reveal sappy sweet in its place? Just for the case of dog food riding in my trailer?" He punches my arm and it stings, but only a little.

"Hey!" I say. "I'm not the one who did the bidding. Who got sappy first?"

"I guess I had rocks in my head," he says.

But he's smiling like an outlaw as he slips a CD in the car stereo. Willie Nelson never sounded so good.

Unloading is easier than loading was. The little Buckskin is more than ready to get out and pushes back the minute the trailer gate opens. That's good, as long as she doesn't panic and twist an ankle—or worse, run away. If she bolted, it could take days to find her.

I snatch up the lead the minute she's out and dangle an open bag of apples—a peace offering—to distract her. She's tired, so she doesn't resist. "Smart horse," I say.

"What's *that*?" Peggy yells from atop her giant grey Thoroughbred. Jinx was an Olympic dressage champion before Peggy's father bought him. His real name is Imperial's Silver Jinx, and I'd need a stepladder to climb into his saddle. But Peggy the teen queen would never let me ride him anyway. To her I'm just "the help." She's not that even much older than I am. What a pain.

"Don't let her bait you this time," Jack says.

I nod. "It's my new horse."

"Looks a bit small to be a horse," Peggy says. "She could be a cute little lead pony for Jinx, I guess. What do you say, Jinx, would you like a pet?"

We all know the answer to that question. Jinx bullies all of the other horses. He's pastured alone when he grazes. No one will even rent the stall next to his.

"Speaking of lead," Jack interrupts, "lead her to the empty paddock, the strong, metal one."

I'm a little nervous. What if she tries to run? But Jack thinks it's okay, so I trust him. "Should I take the halter off, once I get her in there?" I ask.

Peggy rolls her eyes. "Dumb and dumber," she says.

Jack ignores her. "Yup," he answers me. "Her lessons begin tomorrow morning—and so do yours. But tonight, she gets to relax."

"*That* should be fun," Peggy says as she

tethers Jinx to the rail and walks to her chauffeured Imperial Enterprises Town Car. "Annie, give him a good rubdown when you're done playing *Little Pony.* A star like Jinx deserves the best."

I don't answer, but she knows I'll get it done. I've worked for Jack and boarders like Peggy since we moved here about a year ago. Well, I'm only fourteen, so technically I volunteer in exchange for riding lessons. But boarders slip me cash to get out of chores they'd rather not do.

It's the only way a girl like me can afford to horse around, especially at a place like this. Top Tier Stable is the Neiman Marcus of Colorado equestrian clubs, and I can barely afford K-Mart. But today I feel rich. She's not corporate-owned like Jinx, but this horse is all mine.

"Who drives that car anyway?" I ask.

"Don't you have better things to do than wonder about Peggy's chauffeur?"

He has a point, but everything about her puzzles me. She has it all: beauty, money, a world champion horse. Why does she have it out for me? Most days, I'd obsess on that. But Jack is right. Today is not "most days."

I walk my Buckskin to the paddock and open the gate. She eats an apple slice after we walk through. I close the gate behind us and slip her halter off, but she's so beat, she barely reacts. My heart hurts a little. I squeeze through the top and middle rungs of the fence and stand on the bottom rail. She eats the last apple, snorts in my empty hand, and walks away.

"See you tomorrow," I say, as Jack tosses a leaf of alfalfa hay into the paddock and fills her trough with fresh water. She drinks deeply. It's been a long day, and I know she wants to rest. But a crisp, autumn breeze blows across the foothills.

The little horse turns into the wind and smells something familiar. Like magic, the scent leaves her renewed. In a burst of energy, she gallops across the empty paddock, bucking like crazy. Halfway down she spins around to face me and a loud defiant whinny explodes from her lungs. We are electrified—the both of us.

"I own a horse," I say softly, "a wild little Buckskin Mustang." Then I start to worry. What if she's afraid while I'm gone?

"I'm never far," Jack says pointing to the house up the hill. "Her pen is closer to my place than the barn. If she needs me, I'm a heartbeat away."

"Thanks," I tell him, "for everything."

I've never been happier, but a tug-of-war is about to begin.

CHAPTER THREE
Girl Versus Horse

My alarm rings at 7:00 a.m. I slip on my jeans, a t-shirt, and my old cowboy boots. I'm craving bacon, but I choke down a bowl of Raisin Bran—Mom likes things healthy these days. I grab an apple and string cheese for lunch, but I would eat paper if it would get me to the stable faster.

"Feed Abbey before you leave," Mom says. She's working on her latest book. She could feed the dog later, but insists I'm still responsible for my "first horse"—a Great Dane. So I empty the kibble bag into the bowl and top off her water.

"I'll walk you when I get home," I say as I hug her spotted neck. Then I'm off. I don't catch the school bus; I catch a ride to the barn. I've been homeschooled since we moved to Colorado, and I used to hate it. Try making real friends when the only kids you know are online. But all that has changed.

The fact that my schedule is flexible now is ideal. I work at the stable in the morning, walk Abbey before dinner, and do my schoolwork after dark. Perfect, since I have a new horse to school.

I am thinking of names by the time my stepdad, Jeff, drops me off at the Top Tier office. Jack likes Little Bit. "You can call her Bitty, for short," he says. But I think that sounds old-fashioned.

"We could call her Blaze for the mark on her face," I say.

"You'd have to call her Baldy," Jack says. I shoot him a dirty look, but he just laughs.

"What about Poco?" Jeff says. "It's Spanish for little."

Jeff knows nothing about horses. He's a reporter for the *Denver Post*, and his favorite animal is a snake. But he loves my mom and me. And he feels a little guilty for making us move, so he helps me whenever he can, however he can. A reporter's schedule is flexible, too.

I did a report on wild horses. They're not really wild. Early humans hunted horses into extinction in North America long ago. But Spanish conquistadors brought hearty little mustangs back to the Americas in the 1500s. When they escaped, they formed the herds that still roam our wilderness today. So Poco feels right.

"Good job, Jeff," I say. He pats himself on the back and says he'll pick me up at 4:00 p.m. Then he heads off to interview a hero or a criminal, whatever he's investigating today. "Don't forget to buy dog food!" I yell, but I have no idea if he hears.

"I like it," Jack says. "Poco. Good name. Now get a halter on the beast and meet me at the hitching rail outside the barn. I'll gather the things we need."

We walk through the barn, and I notice four plastic owls on the rafters. "What are those," I ask, "and why are they up there?"

"Just trying to class the place up," Jack says. "Maybe scare away a few mice."

"Class?" I say. "I like the barn cats better." Jack shrugs and keeps walking, so I head for the paddock outside. I feel butterflies in my stomach when I see Poco lying in the dust, just soaking up the morning sun. An autumn breeze scatters her mane, but her coat isn't too dirty. With a good brushing, I might be able to make it shine. I can't wait to try.

She sees me and gets to her feet. "Hello Poco," I call softly. I pull a carrot from my pocket. "Want a treat?" I ask, but her eyes are locked on the red halter in my other hand. "Come on," I say. "You're not afraid of this, are you? A tough little horse like you?"

Poco snorts and scrapes her front hoof on the ground, then she slowly walks toward me. She's still looking at the halter, but she smells the sweet scent of carrot. It distracts her, so I let her take it from my hand. As she crunches the orange goodness, she begins to sniff the halter, but I pretend not to notice.

"Easy," Jack says from outside the paddock. "Give her all the time she needs to give you permission."

Deep breaths move in and out of Poco's lungs. She flares her nostrils, exploring the odd thing they'd slipped on her head the day before. Once she's had time to smell it, I move it up toward her head, and rub it gently against her neck.

"See?" I say. "It doesn't hurt." She seems calm, so I guide her nose through the crown piece and toward the strap that will rest across her nose. Her ears go back, but she's not moving. "Good," I whisper. "Now your ears."

One ear slips behind the crown piece easily, and I think I'm home free. I glance back, smiling at Jack. His eyes open wide, just before I go horizontal. Poco jerks back to dodge the halter, then leaps forward, knocking me to the ground like a rag doll.

"You okay?" Jack says, laughing. "Guess she gave you the slip. Tough little cookie, that one."

"So am I," I answer. She wins three more rounds, but by the fourth, the wrestling has ended. Poco is wearing the halter, and our challenge has begun. I want to brush the mud from her coat, so we walk her up to the barn where the supplies are stored. I move to tie her to the rail, but Jack shakes his head.

"Tie her up, and she might panic," he says. "I'll hold the lead while you make her shine." I pick up a grooming brush and try to run the firm bristles down Poco's neck, but she sidesteps my touch. I am confused.

"It's new to her," Jack says. "She doesn't know what it is. Let her smell it."

It feels ridiculous, but I hold the brush in front of her nose. She takes a deep sniff and mouths it with her lips. "You can't eat it," I say, but she's already drawn the same conclusion. She shakes her head and calmly looks away. Stroke by stroke, I brush the coat of a horse that has never before been brushed. Imagine that.

With each grooming tool, we follow the same steps. Show, smell, clean. Show, smell, clean. An hour later, her transformation has begun. Her mane is trimmed and the prairie mud is all gone from nose to tail. I feel victorious, and say, "I *am* the Horse Whisperer."

"Yeah sure," Jack says. "Let's see you whisper with a horse blanket."

I take the thick pad of cloth and walk toward Poco. But I move too quickly, and she jumps back. Jack reels in the slack of the lead rope and whispers, "Steady girl, easy." His confidence calms her so he tells me, "Start again."

This time, I let her see the blanket. I let her explore it with her nose and her mouth. "It's okay," I whisper, "no teeth, no danger, just fabric." To my relief, Poco lets me slide it up and over her back. She's worried, but holding. I'm ready to try the saddle, but Jack eases me back too.

"It's late," he says, "and we should end on a high note, so let's call it a day."

I agree, and I know we've done pretty well, but it seems so slow. I'm a little frustrated. As we walk her to the paddock, I ask, "Is there a quicker way?"

"Do you want to do it fast," he says, "or do you want to do it right?"

"Can't we do both?" I say.

"Not if you want Poco to trust you," he says, petting her neck firmly. Poco leans into his touch, and I feel a little jealous. "She doesn't understand any of this," he says. "She's been taken from her home, she's been poked and prodded, and worse, she's lost her freedom. How would you feel?"

I don't have to wonder. My heart broke into a hundred pieces when we moved to Colorado. I lost my home, my friends, even my confidence. I know exactly how she feels.

One day she's galloping across the prairie with her friends, the next a flying monster is chasing her. It forces her to run for miles. When she can no longer run, when she's so tired she can hardly walk, it lands and a swarm of people spill out. They yell, they swing ropes, they force her onto a truck with fifty other horses. The life she loved is gone.

I weave my fingers through Poco's mane.

"Train her gentle," Jack whispers, "and she'll be your friend for life. Do it fast and you'll break her spirit and her heart. It's your choice."

"No choice at all," I say. We'll take it slow.

And someday, the fear in Poco's eyes will be replaced with hope. From now on, we're in this together. From now on, we're a team.

I carefully put the tack away and walk Poco to the paddock. Jack walks with us.

"Think we're forming a bond?" I ask.

"Let's hope so," he says, "because tomorrow, you ride."

CHAPTER FOUR
Rain, Rain Go Away

That night I dream of Poco and me, galloping bareback through the wilderness, two creatures totally in sync. There is no need for a saddle or a bridle. Poco reads my mind. I squeeze gently with my right leg, she moves to the left. I squeeze with my left she moves to the right. I say whoa, and she slides to a stop.

It is bliss until we hear the thunder. Hundreds of horses suddenly surround us. They gallop at full speed in a panic. Poco's instincts tell her to run, too. But she can feel my fear, and she's torn. Serve her friend or her nature? It is not an easy choice.

As we dodge and swerve to escape the last of the runners, a stallion appears—a towering Dun the color of flame. I wonder why he's at the rear of his herd instead of at the lead as I watch him gallop toward us. Each stride is defiant. There is anger in his eyes.

Poco cries out as he slides to a stop. Dust clouds our vision, but Poco stands her ground. The stallion rears and then nips Poco on her haunches. He commands her to follow the herd, but she refuses. Enraged, the Dun lays his ears back and lowers his head.

My cry wakes me, just before the stallion strikes, and I'm glad it was only a dream. But my heart is still pounding. I can't sleep, and it's way too early to go to the stable. So I start rereading *Black Beauty* for the twentieth time. I fall asleep just before my alarm rings. It's going to be a long day.

It's pouring when Jeff drops me off at the stable. I braid my hair and slip on a sweatshirt to ward off the cold. I walk to the office in the back of the barn and see Jack talking on the phone. He looks as cloudy as the sky when he hangs up.

"Did you leave Peggy Stockton's saddle out last night?" he asks. I can feel the heat of my face turning red.

"I did not," I say, more forcefully than I mean to. It's like I've been punched in the stomach.

"Her $3000 show saddle was drenched on the hitching post when I got here," Jack says. "I just talked to her dad, Lex. Peggy says you promised to put it away."

"What is her problem?" I say. "She has it out for me. She always has."

"Cut her some slack," Jack says. "She doesn't have it easy."

"Her father is richer than God, and she gets everything she wants," I say. "How does she NOT have it easy?"

"You don't know the whole story," Jack says. "You'll just have to trust me on that."

I don't know what to say, so I shake my head and sink into the office chair. My safety zone is dissolving before my eyes.

"Settle down," Jack tells me. "Peggy's dad is on the Top Tier board of directors so I had to ask. But anyone could have done this, including Peggy. When has she ever taken responsibility for her mistakes?"

Never is the only word that comes to mind, but I stay quiet. It's my head on the chopping block, not hers.

"I'll get my things," I whisper, wondering what will happen to Poco now that I can't earn her keep. I fight back the tears in my eyes.

"Did I not tell you to settle down?" Jack says. "You're not fired. You're my right arm volunteer around here. Besides, who'd train that mustang with you gone?" He gives me a proper hug. "You're not going anywhere, and neither am I. Worst case scenario, we replace the saddle."

Who has $3000 sitting around collecting dust? It might as well be $3 million. But I make the only offer I can. "I've got $156 left," I say, "and Poco may never need a saddle. It's yours."

"Not going to happen," Jack interrupts. "We'll find another way. Maybe Lex has insurance and Poco takes a saddle just fine." Jack's mind is made up, so there is no point in arguing. But it's not his fault any more than it's mine.

"Now," Jack says. "Get that wet horse of yours. It's too muddy to work with her outside. Might as well introduce her to her indoor accommodations."

Jack reads the surprise on my face. We both know I can't afford a stall. "Consider it an employee perk," he says, waving his arm like a magician. That's when I see it—Poco's name engraved on a Top Tier stall—right next door to Jinx's. That explains the bargain. I wonder how often Jinx will bite Poco, but get serious. A free stall next to Godzilla beats the sting of a snowy pasture. I can't wait to bring her in from the rain.

Poco is a sight, standing soaked in the paddock. Covered in mud, she hasn't been standing for long. She doesn't resists when I slip on her halter and we walk to the barn with ease. But she pauses when we get to the open stable doors. She is worried, until she sees Jack.

"Well, look what the cat drug in," Jack says, walking toward Poco. "Ready for civilization?" He scratches her under her chin, and her fear eases. "May I?" he says, reaching for her lead. I don't resist either.

Speaking softly, almost hypnotically, Jack leads her toward the stall. Every stall in the barn has a private, outdoor paddock. Luxury barn, luxury perks. The door from her stall to her paddock is closed, but the floor inside is lined with fresh straw. The water bucket is filled; there is hay in her feeder, and sweet grain is waiting in a big, metal bucket. "Check out your new digs," he says. Poco follows him in without a trace of hesitation.

It's quiet in the barn. No one else is around, so when Jinx kicks the wall of his stall, I jump like a jackrabbit. Jack laughs. "He smells the sweet grain—oats, corn, and molasses," Jack says. Jinx smells Poco, too, and whinnies. Poco's eyes widen, and she answers. It's as close as she's been to another horse since the auction. I want to warn her, Jinx is not her friend. But time will be her teacher.

"Pick up the bucket," Jack tells me. "Give her a taste." One bite and Poco forgets there is anything in the world but food. She's never had anything so delicious. "Home sweet home," Jack says, and from the way she's eating, it's clear Poco agrees.

We decide to give her a little time alone while staying close by to keep an eye on her. Some horses panic in small spaces, and Poco's a wild card.

"Let's take a closer look at Peggy's saddle," Jack says. I am hoping it's just a little damp, but the pricy Stubben Jack carries on his arm is still dripping wet.

"Can we save it?" I ask. Poco calls to Jinx, and, this time, he responds. I wonder what they're saying.

"Some people cure their leather in the bathtub," he says. "I can't see Lex being satisfied with that. He'll want something new, but we'll salvage it just the same. If we can stop mold from setting in, someone will want it."

Makes me wish I rode English like Peggy. She looks so sophisticated in her khaki jodhpurs and black show jacket. Even her tall, black boots and helmet look expensive. And, of course, they are.

"Would a hot blow dryer help dry the saddle?" I ask.

"Only if you want the leather to crack," he says. I wonder if there is anything Jack doesn't know about horses and riding. "We'll towel if off as best we can, then air dry it with a fan for a couple of weeks. With a little luck, some patience, and a lot of leather conditioner, it's possible."

We go through half a dozen towels, then place the damp saddle on a barrel shaped rack to help it hold its shape. We move the rack into the stable office at the back of the barn. "Climate controlled," Jack says smiling, "better for the leather. We'll start conditioning it with leather treatment tomorrow."

"Manley!" A deep, angry voice thunders through the barn, and though we've never met, I know it has to be Lex Stockton. Jinx lays his ears back and tries to bite the big man's arm as he walks by. I brace for what he is about to say, but nothing could have prepared me. When he bursts through the office door, Peggy is with him.

"That's her," Peggy whimpers. Her face is swollen, and I can tell she's been crying. "She left the saddle outside. I wouldn't. . . . " Peggy winces as her father's hand closes around the flesh of her arm. She's wearing what looks like a nightgown. Mud covers her sneakers, and she shivers under a paper-thin Imperial Enterprises windbreaker.

"Who owns the saddle?" Stockton says through gritted teeth, staring at Jack, not Peggy. He is winded from the short walk through the stable. His face is ruby red.

"We do," she whispers.

"That's right," he continues. "Who should have put the saddle away?"

"She promised," Peggy says. Her father's fingers sink deeper into her arm, and she cries out. They remind me of a falcon's claws.

"Who SHOULD have put it away?" he repeats.

"I should have," Peggy surrenders.

"And?" her father releases her arm with a shove. I wonder how bruised she is underneath.

"I am a disappointment," she says. Tears streak her cheeks.

"And?" he repeats, still staring in Jack's eyes.

"I'll earn every penny to replace it."

"See that she does," Stockton tells Jack, "or Jinx and the rest of my equine investments are history."

Stockton storms out of the office and down the middle of the stable so quickly, Peggy has to run to keep up. It all happens so fast, neither Jack nor I have a chance to utter a peep.

"Like I said," Jack finally breaks the silence, "she doesn't have it easy."

This time I agree.

CHAPTER FIVE
Beginner's Luck

A note from Peggy is tacked to Poco's stall the next morning.

"You got me in trouble," it says, "but I WILL get you back."

My stomach is in knots. It's not guilt. We both know I didn't leave her saddle out. But after seeing her dad Hulk out, I feel sick. Mom says my dad was just as bad, but I never knew him. If Mom hadn't left, if Jeff hadn't stepped up, I might be in Peggy's shoes.

"Remind me to give Mom and Jeff a hug," I say to Poco as I open the stall door to refill her water trough. She hangs her head over the door to nuzzle Jinx. I'm amazed he doesn't sink his teeth into her. They say the scars he's left are legendary.

"I'll remind you," Jack says in a high-pitched falsetto.

"Very funny," I say. "But you sound nothing like her."

"How do you know," he says in the same voice, "have you ever heard her talk?"

I shake my head. Old guys are weird.

"Peggy writing you love letters?" he says, ripping the note from the stall. "Tell me you didn't let this get to you."

"I didn't," I say. "But what's with her dad? I kind of feel sorry for her."

"Divorce and money," Jack says. "Some rich people go Robin Hood, some go Prince John."

"Am I supposed to understand that?" I say.

"You don't read?" he asks. "No classics?" I

stare. “Okay, some people get rich and share what they have, right? Others think they never have enough and get mad. Lex is the angry type.”

“Must be exhausting,” I say. Jack nods.

“Gather your horse,” he says. “It’s time to try a saddle.”

Poco now wears a halter like a pro, so I slip it on her, brush down her coat and walk her to the wooden exercise ring outside the barn—cool, calm, and collected. I close the gate behind us and head toward Jack at the center. An old saddle and saddle pad are leaning against his leg, and a bridle is in his hand. Jinx watches from his outdoor paddock.

“Hold the lead,” Jack says, “but give her a little room.” He’s taking charge, and I’m glad. I’m too short to be as gentle as I should be. When I saddle a horse, it’s like a twenty-five pound surprise. With Jack, it’s a dance.

He checks the padded horse blanket for hitch hikers—sticks, stones, or burrs that might cause Poco pain beneath the weight of a rider. Then he presents it to her like a gift, and, after a few sniffs, she accepts. Jack lays it softly on the top of her back. "Good girl," he whispers. She listens to his reassuring tone.

Jack lifts the saddle and hooks the right stirrup over the saddle horn. He drapes the cinches over the seat of the saddle, too. Poco sees him in her peripheral vision and sidesteps to gain a little distance, but Jack reads the motion and matches it. "No worries," he whispers, and lowers the saddle for her inspection. Once she calms to it, he continues. He lifts the saddle and gently places it on the center of her back over the pad.

Poco flinches and muscle ripple beneath her skin. But she doesn't run. She reads trust in Jack's eyes and trusts him in return, even as he tightens both cinches around her belly. "Bridle," he says like a doctor doing surgery, and I deliver it with my free hand. The ringed, silver snaffle bit glistens in the sun.

I've heard a snaffle is gentler on a horse's mouth than other, stiffer bits, and Jack confirms it. "This won't hurt her too much," he says as he dangles it in front of her, "if you don't pull too hard." His eyes lock on mine. "Do NOT pull hard."

I nod as he smiles, wraps his right arm around Poco's head, and guides the bridle toward her face. Cheek to cheek, they stand staring at me when Jack starts to sing, softly. So softly I can only hear something about dancing and night.

"Orleans," he whispers, naming the oldies band he's humming as he slides the bit into Poco's mouth and fastens the bridle strap around her jaw. "God love the 70s."

He turns to face Poco, stroking her nose as he sings on. His singing is still so soft that I can't hear any words, and then his singing slips back into humming.

"Music soothes the savage beast," he whispers and continues to hum. He slips his left boot in the left stirrup of Poco's saddle. His body rises gracefully until all his weight is on one side of the saddle. Then slowly, even tenderly, he drapes his body across the seat, like a two hundred pound sack of singing beans.

"She isn't fighting it," I say. "And she's playing with the snaffle against her tongue." I am amazed. I see no fear.

"Atta girl," Jack says, sliding off of Poco's back. He scratches under her jaw and she drinks in his approval. I should be pleased, but I'm not. I'm jealous.

"Can I try?" I ask, and Jack nods.

"Take it slow," he says. "It's about trust."

He's right, but I don't hear a word. All I can hear is the sound of my heart pounding—the sound of my insecure thoughts. *I have to make her love me*, I am thinking. But my approach is dead wrong.

Poco hears my boots rushing toward her. Her ears go back—a warning I ignore. I lift my left foot into the left stirrup, as Jack did, but I do not pause to prepare her. I throw my right leg over the saddle and shove my foot into the stirrup. I am not smart as I kick my wild Mustang in the side.

My shy little Buckskin, so new to the world of people, panics. A reckless creature is in her saddle, an unyielding bit is in her mouth, and a thick, wooden fence has her captured. I pull back on the reins, begging her to stop. But "stop" isn't a word she's learned yet, and with every tug the bit cuts into the back of her tender mouth and hurts her more. Instinct tells her to escape the pain, so she does. Three out of four wooden rails snap like twigs when Poco hits them at a gallop, and I am suddenly airborne.

Poco runs for the safety of the barn, to Jinx in his outdoor paddock for reassurance, as I sit in mud outside the ring. The Thoroughbred cries out as if he's defending her. I should be ashamed he's a better ally than I am, but I'm not. I'm too mad.

"Stupid horse," I say, brushing mud from the scrapes on my elbows.

"Stupid horse?" Jack asks. I am not the only one who is angry. "What in the holy heavens were you doing, Annie? Did you leave your brain under your pillow?"

He blows past me without offering a hand up. He gives Jinx a pat over the metal bars of the pen then gathers Poco's reins and tries to calm her. As the big horse nuzzles her, he checks Poco's legs and chest for cuts and swelling, then leads her back to the outside of the ring.

"Get up," he says. I stand slowly. I've never seen him like this before, but I know better than to speak. I stare at the mud on my boots.

"Get on," Jack says.

"Are you crazy?" I say. "She nearly killed me."

"YOU nearly killed HER," Jack snaps, "jumping on her back like she was an old nag for babies and grandmas. Digging your heels into her side. Driving her through the fence. You think she hurt you? You're lucky she's not lame, slamming against those boards."

I am quiet as the reality of my behavior sinks in.

"You've got to fix this," he says. "Undo the damage you did."

"How?" I question him, and myself. Not a scrap of confidence survived the collision.

"You scared her to death," Jack says, "and worse, you let a green horse prove she was the boss. If you don't fix that now, you can forget ever being a team."

I worry about her bolting again, about her jumping the last wooden rail, about what people watching us might think. But losing Jack's respect worries me more. So I do exactly as he says.

Poco is still breathing hard. She is still afraid of me and the exercise ring. But after three failed attempts and two more falls in the mud, she finally jumps over the bottom rung back into the exercise ring. I smile when we succeed, but Jack does not.

"You're done for today," he says. "Go call you parents."

I walk to the barn alone as Jack tends to Poco in the ring. I try not to cry, but it's impossible. I let my horse and my only friend down, and now I have to explain it to my parents. I can't think of a better reason to cry.

When Jeff rolls up, Jack leads Poco to the driver's side and talks to him for a few minutes while I gather my things. They laugh and shake hands, but Jack doesn't look at me. I wish he would. I want to say I'm sorry, but he's like granite. He turns and walks Poco to the barn as I climb into the car. I wipe tears from my face with my sleeve.

"Tomorrow," he calls over his shoulder, "You listen to me. Are we clear?"

"We're clear," I say.

"And tomorrow," he continues, "you mend the broken fence."

Jack is too far away to hear, but I say it anyway. "I'll make this right."

"Sounds like a rough one," Jeff says, and squeezes my hand.

The rest of the drive home is quiet, but I'm glad. There's nothing good left to say. I spend the rest of the night in my room. And when I sleep, not a dream comes to mind. I'm grateful for that, too.

CHAPTER SIX
Mending Fences

“I hear you have chores to do,” Peggy says when I get to the stable with lumber and tools. I have chores every day, and she knows it. But it’s hard to miss the shattered rails, and bad news travels fast.

“Nothing new,” I say walking past her toward the ring. We both know that’s a lie.

“I would have paid a lot of money to watch you fly,” she says, laughing. She grabs Jinx by the mane and swings up on him, bareback.

They head for the open pasture for an autumn run, just as I pound in the very first nail.

An hour later, Peggy is back to catch her fancy ride home, and the new slats are up on the old posts. If the boards weren't so fresh, you would hardly notice the difference. I gather the tools and carry them back to the office where Jack sits behind his desk.

"You finished?" he asks, and I nod without a word. He walks to the office window to evaluate my work. I hope I see him smile, but I'm not sure. Or maybe I'm afraid to look. "C'mon," he says. We walk to Poco's stall to find her and Jinx standing head to head.

"Glad you finally found a friend," Jack says.

"I'm Poco's friend too," I whisper. I try not to cry, but it's not working. We walk two steps, and the sniffles begin.

"Take a breath," he says, finally putting his arm around my shoulders. "You will do better today, right?"

I nod, relieved that I am forgiven. Then the

floodgates fall, but we keep walking.

"Besides," he says as he as he moves ahead of me, "I was talking to Jinx."

"Can we try it again?" I ask. Jack picks up the old saddle and heads for the ring I just repaired. I have my answer.

Poco is not eager to repeat our recent history, and neither am I. But Jack is right. I have to fix what I've broken. I have to win back Poco's trust.

"Let's go back to square one," I say. I pull a bag of apple slices from my pocket, but Poco turns away. I'm pretty sure I deserve that, but we walk on.

Jack opens the gate and takes Poco's lead. Good strategy, I think. He didn't cause her pain, so he should bring her in. Once we reach the center of the ring, Jack says it's my turn, and I know exactly what to do.

It's time to prove who I really am—or at least who I want to be. So I speak softly, lovingly, as I offer her the apple slice again.

This time, she doesn't refuse. I lay my head against her neck and whisper thank you. I get a lump in my throat when she leans back.

"There we go," Jack says. "Horses always know the good guys." It may be the nicest thing he's ever said. We put on her saddle and bridle and, eventually, she lets me climb on. I settle gently into the seat, then we walk. Jack holds the reins at first. We circle the ring a couple of times. Then he hands the reins back to me.

"Slow and easy," he says. "Keep it up while I check on the barn."

"Should I try a little trot?" I ask.

"Poco will let you know," he says. "But be gentle with the bit. Her mouth is tender from yesterday, and you don't want to cause her more pain." I nod, but he can see I'm worried. "Don't look so scared," he says. "I wouldn't leave you if I didn't think you could handle it."

Being alone with Poco frightens me. But she is my horse. She's four years old, and I'm fourteen. We could be together another twenty years, if we're lucky. So we have to come to an understanding. It starts with this walk—around and around and around. And we talk a little as we go.

"You have a right to be mad at me," I say. Her ears swivel back to listen. I know she doesn't understand the words, but she can read my tone, and it's different. "I was wrong to rush you yesterday, but I promise never to do it again." She shakes her head, but she's not arguing. The wind is just tickling her ears.

"I will make other mistakes," I continue. "But I will never be jealous again. I know why you love Jack. We're lucky to have him to teach us. If I work hard, he'll show me how to earn your love. So I WILL work hard."

With every pass around the ring, my mood lifts and I wonder if she feels the same. "Do you want to try a trot?" I ask, and I hope her answer is yes. I do not kick. I gently squeeze with my legs, and like magic, she begins to trot. I feel triumphant for the first time in days, like I just won the blue ribbon. Then I ease her back to a walk and climb off.

"What are you grinning about?" Jack says walking back into the ring. I don't know what to say, so I just keep smiling. He ruffles my hair like I'm a puppy. Sometimes being happy is enough. Poco and I had a good day, and Jack is back on my side. Or maybe I'm back on his.

"Get back on and ride her up to the barn," he says. "You've earned a victory lap."

That's an easy ride. Even wild Mustangs run toward the barn when they're hungry. She might stop to flirt with Jinx on the way up, but that's okay. They really have become an odd little couple. But he's not in his paddock, so she heads right up to the barn. I slip her saddle and bridle off and look toward her stall. I can't see Jinx inside the barn, either.

"Where's Jinx?" I ask, and guesses fly—maybe he's on a trail ride, maybe he's in the pasture, maybe he's at the vet. No one really knows, but no one is worried, either, until I put Poco away and make a troubling discovery. The slide latch on Jinx's stall isn't just unlocked. It's lying on the ground.

CHAPTER SEVEN
Lost and Found

Jack calls Lex Stockton, and it's official. No one took Jinx from the barn, and they haven't seen him since Peggy left the stable around noon. Jack says his next call will be to the police. Stealing a five-figure Thoroughbred is a crime.

But Lex is adamant. "No police," he says. "We'll handle this matter in house."

"Sure you will," Jack says to the dial tone. But he's not satisfied. He decides to search for

Jinx on his own. "Can you stick around for a while?" he asks. "I need someone to sit by the phones." I say yes, but he doesn't wait to hear it. He saddles his horse Buckeye and heads for the doors.

Jack mounts Buckeye like a Hollywood cowboy, and I wonder, was he ever considered handsome? Something tells me he probably was.

"I've got my cell phone," he hollers. "Call me if Jinx turns up."

Losing a horse in Colorado in daylight is bad. Losing a horse in Colorado after dark is worse. Temperatures drop, terrain gets hard to navigate, and lately wolves have been making themselves known.

A pack killed an old sheep on the ranch next door. And at night we hear howling from the hills. Most packs won't take on a horse as big as Jinx. But if he's hurt or disoriented, things could go terribly wrong.

I call my mom to ask her to walk Abbey. I call Jeff so he won't swing by at 4:00 p.m. And

I call Pizza Shack, because Jack will be hungry when he gets back. I'm just locking up when Peggy's town car appears at the doors and, of course, I let her in.

"Did you do this?" she asks. It's more accusation than question.

"Of course not," I say. "I love Jinx. So does Poco."

"It's her fault," Peggy says. "She's so wild, she made him wander."

"That's just stupid," I say. "It's not like they have secret conversations. Get serious."

"Shut up," she says, "your kind knows nothing." Normally, that would make me mad, but she's trying not to cry, and I know her parents are split up. I can't be annoyed and feel sorry for her at the same time. So sorry wins out.

"What do we know about what happened?" she asks.

"We know Jinx got out some time before 3:00 p.m. this afternoon," I say. "That's when

I noticed he was gone. But look at this." I lead her back to the stall and show her the broken latch. "It's not just broken, it's destroyed. Someone did this on purpose."

"Who would do that?" she asks.

"I have no idea," I say. "But we have a better chance if we trust Jack to find out."

Peggy is quiet. She runs her fingers across the broken wood and leans her head on Jinx's nameplate. "Okay," she says. "But we have to find Jinx. And I'm not going home until we do."

"Agreed," I say. "Jack's got a couple of sleeping bags in the office. I'll get them. It's going to be a long, long night if he isn't back soon." When I get back to the stalls with the bags, the pizza delivery guy is outside. I pay for the food out of petty cash and bring it inside, but neither one of us is hungry.

Peggy spends the next few hours on her smartphone, and I read a book I found collecting dust. Jack and Buckeye are back by midnight, but there's still no sign of Jinx. He grabs a slice and a soda and sits down beside us.

"Peggy, we'll find him," he says. "I'll be back out on the trail at first light. And I'll sleep in the barn in case he shows up. You two can call your folks and head home."

"We're not going anywhere," Peggy says. She looks to me for backup.

"That's right," I say. "We're in this together. We'll be able to sleep after he's found." Jack can see this is locked in, so he gives up without a fight.

"Your parents approve?" he says. We nod. "A sleepover it is. But I'm old, so I get the office couch."

Peggy and I slip into the bags and settle down for the night. We are surrounded by twenty-four sleeping horses, two cats, and one empty space. I can hear the animals breathing, but the saddest sound is Peggy's muffled sob. For the first time, I can see it. She needs Jinx as much as I need Poco. We've got to bring her best friend home.

Sleeping on the dirt floor of the stable is nearly impossible, but as I start to drift off, I hear Poco nickering. I lift my head, and she bumps it up a notch. She starts to neigh, then whinny. "Easy girl," I whisper. "You're going to wake the whole stable." But it's too late to quiet her. Something is on her mind, and she's not going to stop. So I decide to investigate.

I tiptoe into Jack's office to peek out the window. "Thank goodness," I whisper. Jinx is standing outside.

"Indeed," Jack says softly. I should have known he'd wake up. I turn around to give him a high five, but he's not celebrating. "He's not alone," Jack says.

I turn back to the window. A massive wolf has Jinx cornered.

"Stay here," Jack says, grabbing his baseball bat, but we run through the stable together.

Peggy wakes and yells, "What's happening?" But there's no time to answer.

Just as we get outside, Jinx rears up to

defend himself. The yelps of a wolf in distress prove he has hit his mark. The battered canine runs for cover, and Jack leads the traumatized horse inside.

"Get the first aid kit," he says, and I run to the office to retrieve it. Blood flows from a deep cut on the horse's dappled chest. Peggy looks on, as white as a stone.

"Is he wolf bit?" she whispers. "Will I lose my horse to rabies?"

"It wasn't the wolf," Jack says. "The cut is too clean. It must have been barbed wire. He was smart enough to head home, but the smell of blood probably drew the wolf." If he hadn't come home, we wouldn't have found his bones until spring. A pack of wolves can easily take down a wounded horse.

I'm on the phone to the vet before Jack can ask me to make the call, but he shouts out a reminder. "Tell her to bring a needle and thread." A few hours later, Jinx has forty-six stitches and a bottle of antibiotics. "He'll be on easy duty for a few weeks," Jack says. "But he'll be okay." He leads Jinx back into his stall and ties it shut with a stretch of chain and a metal stake until the latch is repaired.

Peggy is relieved but out for blood of her own. "Find out who did this," she says as the car pulls up to take her home. "I want someone to pay for every stitch. Can you do that, Jack?"

"I've got a few tricks up my sleeve," he says.

"Let's hope so," she says. "But don't forget my father's instructions."

"Imperial justice," he says.

"Exactly," she agrees. "You take care of Jinx, and my father will take care of the lowlife."

"That's a plan," Jack says as her car drives away.

"Not a good one," I say.

"No worries," he says. "I've got plans of my own."

"Isn't Lex Stockton your boss?" I ask.

"He is on the board of directors," Jack replies, "but he is not my boss. I have to listen to his suggestions, but I never have to do what he says."

"So what's your plan?" I ask.

"We know it happened between noon and 3:00 p.m., right?" he says.

"Check," I say.

"And we know it has to be an inside job."

"Wait a minute," I say. "How do we know that?"

"Someone walked in, pounded off the latch, and left without a single person noticing. Wouldn't you have noticed a stranger with a strange car?"

I hadn't thought of that, but now that he mentions it, it makes sense. "So let's say someone we know did let Jinx out. Who might have it in for a horse?"

"Maybe they didn't have it in for Jinx. Maybe they had it in for Peggy," he says. "Maybe you did it."

"Very funny," I say. Then it hits me. "Maybe someone had it in for Peggy's dad!"

"Now you're thinking," he says. "Here's another question for you. Did you know I installed security cameras inside the barn?"

"You sneaky old cowboy," I say. "When?"

"Couple of days ago. Remember those classy little owls?"

"Those eyesores are cameras?" I say.

Jack nods. "Someone has been dipping into our grain supplies. I want to find out who. They were set to record from 7:00 a.m. to 7:00 p.m., every single day."

"Including yesterday?" I ask.

"Including yesterday," he says. "Whoever perpetrated this crime probably did it in clear view of our feathered friends. All we have to do is find it on the tape and turn it in to the media and the cops. They'll do the rest."

"I don't know any police," I say, "but I do know a reporter we can trust."

"You read my mind," he says. "And you

wonder why I keep you around."

"What about Lex Stockton?" I ask.

"He can read about it in the paper," Jack says. "Now go get some sleep. We'll look over the tape tonight. Bring Jeff, but keep this to yourselves. We want to keep this caper a secret." Since we don't know yet who the person is, that seems like a good idea.

I feel bad that someone tried to hurt Jinx, and I'll be glad when the stable is safe again. But it's strange. All this trouble has made me feel connected to something bigger than myself, like I'm a part of a bigger "we." And that feels pretty great.

CHAPTER EIGHT
Flaming Disaster

"Run that past me again," Jeff says. He can't quite wrap his head around a crime against a horse. Neither can I when it comes to sorting out *why*. But *what*, is crystal clear—at least to me.

"Someone broke the latch on Jinx's stall and probably turned him out to die," I say. "They probably did something to make him run away, and we probably caught it on tape."

"That's not much to go on," he says. "*Probably* isn't a crime, and *probably* isn't proof.

But, sure. I'll help you go over the tape tonight. If you got a shot of the guy's face, I'll pull in my experts to help you make an ID. Fair enough?"

"More than fair," I say. "Let's head over there now."

"Let's eat some dinner first," Jeff says. "Your mom made vegan lasagna, and I can *probably* pretend it's got cheese." Jeff misses real food, too.

By 8:30 p.m., the dishes are washed and we're on our way to Top Tier. Jack says to meet him at his place so we can go over the tape in private. It's an old farmhouse behind the barn, so we take the same dirt road that leads to the stable.

Just before we get to the final turn, we smell smoke. A thick, dark cloud of it floats across the road. We disappear inside the haze and make our way toward the house. "I wonder what's burning," I say. In seconds, I find out.

"Oh my gosh . . ." Jeff says as we pull into

the stable's parking lot. A tiny orange flame is dancing across the back of the barn, but a tower of smoke billows behind it. The fire looks small, but fire has a way of growing up fast.

"JACK!" I scream into my cell phone, "the barn is on fire. You better get here fast."

Jeff is standing by the car, dumbstruck. His mouth falls open, but nothing escapes. "I've got to save them," I say, tossing him my cell phone. "Dial 9-1-1." If he was thinking clearly, he'd tell me not to go. But I wouldn't listen, even if he did.

In seconds, I'm at the barn doors. A warning pops into my head, an old memory from a kindergarten field trip. "Check the door for heat," the fireman told us. "If it's cool, it's safe to open. If it's hot, flames are on the other side. Find another way out."

Or in, I think. I lay the palm of my hand against the wood, and it's still cool. So I throw the doors open wide. Smoke has filled the stable, but the motion sensor is still working.

It reads my movement, and the emergency light snaps on inside. One spotlight at the front of a massive building isn't much help, but it beats utter darkness, especially darkness enveloped in smoke.

I pull the neck of my sweatshirt over my mouth to help me breathe and move cautiously inside. How can I save them all? There are twenty-five horses, and this is all happening so fast. But I block the fear and head for the back of the barn where I first saw the smoke was rising. That end will be the first to go up in flames.

It sounds like a stampede inside, just like my nightmare. It's hot and all the horses are kicking the walls and bugling. I run to Poco's stall first. She's still wearing her halter, and the lead rope is hanging on the door. I throw it open and hook the lead in place. One down, and twenty-four to go. I reach to open the door for Jinx, but a padlock has been added to Jack's temporary chain.

"Who did this?" I scream. But I'm not the only one screaming.

"Get out of the way," Jack says, holding his baseball bat like an all-star. "Help the others. I'll free Jinx and meet you outside." He takes his first swing as I lead Poco to the next stall, and the next, and the next.

I lead Poco and another horse outside where Jeff is standing in awe. "Take them to the exercise ring," I scream, tossing him the ropes. I have no idea if he knows where the exercise ring is, and I know he's never walked a horse, much less two. But I don't have time to explain. I run back into the burning barn to start again.

From back to front, I free them—everything from a million dollar yearling to aging family pets—and pass them off to Jeff, two by two. By the third trip, we're no longer alone. The vet and two other boarders have spotted the smoke and rushed down to give us a hand.

In the end, the heat is overwhelming and embers fall like rain. We can hardly breathe, in or out of the barn, but we can't stop. How can we let a single horse burn?

When we hear the fire trucks coming, twenty-four soot-covered horses are safely corralled in open rings and paddocks. The screams of sirens says a fleet of fire engines will soon handle the fire. People clap as the fire fighters unpack their gear, but there's still no sign of Jack or Jinx. My hope is fading.

As I breathe oxygen from a mask while adults murmur about smoke inhalation, water explodes from the powerful hoses. It vanquishes the flames, but it is a little too late. The barn roof collapses into a heap of blackened splinters, and I feel like I've fallen with it.

"Where are you, Jack?" I say between sobs.

CHAPTER NINE
The Smoke Clears

"Come on," Jeff says, extending his hand to help me up. "It's nearly dawn. All the horses are safe, and it's time to go home."

"Not all the horses," I say, "and not all the cowboys."

"He'll turn up," Jeff says. "He's got nine lives like a cat."

"What if he doesn't?" I say.

"If he doesn't, he went the way he would have wanted to go," Jeff says. "He went fighting for a horse."

I know that should make me feel better, but it doesn't. Jack was just standing beside me. Jinx was standing beside my horse. I don't think I can go home because leaving will make it real. And when I come back, Jack really will be gone.

"Five more minutes," I say. "I need to center my thoughts."

I walk to the large paddock where Poco is corralled. At first she ignores me, distracted by the smoke, the noise, the commotion of other horses. I feel the cool wind against my face. It has started to rain.

"Perfect," I say. "Things couldn't be worse." I start to cry, and Poco's ears turn toward me. She nickers and trots to the rail, as if to comfort me, and I am amazed.

"Of course things could be worse," a falsetto voice says behind me. "A girl and a Buckskin could be ash in that fiery mess." I gasp when I realize that Poco didn't trot over to see *me*.

"Jack!" I scream as I throw my arms around his neck.

"Easy," he says. "Watch the bum arm."

The sleeve is singed on his sweatshirt and the skin underneath is bloody and raw. "You're hurt," I say, "but you're alive. How did you, where did you, Jinx?" I'm afraid of how he'll respond.

"Over there," he nods to the paddock near his house, the pen Poco used her first days here. "I couldn't budge the lock on the chain, so I ran outside to Jinx's private paddock. Ten or twelve bashes with a Louisville slugger and metal bars gave way. I walked him out of the stall, but a section of wood fell from the barn and caught Jinx on the hip. It left a nasty wound, and he'll never grow hair there again, but the Doc says he'll be fine."

"Where were you all this time?" I ask.

"The vet took the back road to the stable," Jack says. "When she saw Jinx and me limping out, she called us over and treated Jinx up at my place. Took a while to patch us up, but here we are, pretty as ever."

"The fire," I ask, "how did it happen?"

Jack's eyes go dark.

"I don't know for sure," he says. "But the fire started by the office where the hay bales were stacked—right next to Jinx's stall. To me, it looks like another hit."

Then I remember. I came down to go over the security tapes. Did our evidence go up in flames? I ask Jack, but he just smiles.

"This is the new millennium," he says. "Surveillance tapes aren't stored in dirty old barns these days. They float right up to the cloud. The stable cameras and laptop are toast. But I've got the footage queued up on the laptop at home."

"Everything is safe?" I say.

"As safe as a movie star's selfies," he laughs, "well, not counting the barn."

"Safer," I say. "Can we search the tapes now?"

"Old guys need their beauty sleep," he says.

"And you've earned a rest after saving twenty-five horses."

"Twenty-four," I say.

"Twenty-five," he repeats. "Last night, we were a team."

"Some team," I say. "Twenty-four to one? You should pay me more."

"I should pay you, period," he replies.

"You're on," I say. "Jeff will bring me back later on."

Falling asleep is nearly impossible, but Mom lays down the law. "No sleep," she says, "no horses." So I lie in my bed until my exhaustion trumps my adrenaline. When I wake up six hours later, Mom is satisfied. So Jeff and I head to Jack's.

We're at it for hours, searching every frame of the video, but finally we hit pay dirt. A man in a black ball cap walks right up to Jinx's stall, crowbars the latch, and drops it in the dust.

"That's one strike," Jeff says, "malicious mischief. Can we can add more charges to his arrest warrant?"

Once the door is open, Jinx wanders casually out of the stall and heads for the grain bin, but the stranger grabs his halter and stops him. His other hand slips into the pocket of his khaki pants and pulls out something shiny. "It's a knife," Jack says.

In one, swift motion, the stranger cuts a three-inch wound in Jinx's chest. "It wasn't barbed wire," I gasp.

"Cruelty to animals," Jeff says. Another charge for the rap sheet. Jack swears under his breath.

Confused and in pain, Jinx runs from the barn. Then we catch a break. The man bends to pick up the crowbar, and we get a clear shot of his face. "Bingo," Jeff says. "That will work for the facial recognition software." But I see something familiar.

"I've seen him!" I shout. "I remember! He was at the auction sitting next to the Butcher. They were laughing."

Jack's head snaps from the computer screen to my face. "Rebecca?" he says. "This guy was sitting with Rebecca?"

I'm a little shocked Jack knows the Butcher's first name, but I shake my head, yes. "I'm sure," I say. "He is wearing the same hat."

"Let's get a closer look at that cap," Jeff says. The logo comes into focus. "Imperial Enterprises? Could this guy work for Peggy's dad?"

Jack excuses himself to make a phone call while Jeff and I save the picture of his face. "I'll email this to my crew at the newspaper," Jeff says. "If he's in the system, we'll have his name by morning."

"We have it now," Jack says. "Rebecca says it's Louis Blackwater. She says he's Lex Stockton's bodyguard and chauffeur."

"Shut up!" I say. "The guy that drives Peggy around?"

"The same," Jack says. "Now let's see if he also started the fire."

CHAPTER TEN
The Swift Arm of Justice

I fall into bed when we get home from Jack's after midnight, but Jeff doesn't. He's too busy gathering facts for his article on the fire. He's just wrapping it up as I come down for breakfast. When he hits send, the email goes to his editor at the *Denver Post*, Jack Manley, and the chief of police for our county.

Jeff is ready to crash, but he offers me a ride to the stable.

“What do you know about Rebecca Travers?” Jeff asks as he drives.

“Only that she buys horses to kill for dog food. Disgusting,” I say.

“Imperial Enterprises, dog food owned by Lex Stockton,” he says. “And what do you think we feed Abbey? Would it interest you to know Rebecca quit that job three years ago to start a wild horse rescue?” I am speechless and a little embarrassed. He continues. “I guess she didn’t like the job, either.”

“How did she know Louis Blackwater?” I ask.

“Blackwater took her place brokering horse meat,” Jeff says, “She had to train him. So he was the Butcher at the auction, and she was salvation. Guess things aren’t always what they seem to be.”

“You can say that again,” I whisper as we pull up to what used to be the stable. Jeff says he’ll pick me up as soon as he gets a little shut-eye. As tired as he is, that may be a week from Friday. But taking care of the horses will keep me busy. I find Jack sorting through the rubble.

"I'm surprised you came down here today," he says. "There's not much left."

Truth is, I can't imagine being anywhere else. The Top Tier barn may be a pile of ash, but it's my home away from home. And Jack needs me more than ever. "Not much to do at home, anyway," I say. "What are you doing?"

"I already stopped by the feed store for temporary provisions. And I fed and watered the horses in the rings and paddocks," he answers. "I guess I'm looking for the silver lining now. They say it's always there, if you know where to look."

"Do you know where to look?" I ask.

"I might," he says. "And I sure won't give up trying."

"How did you know the Butcher?" I ask, "I mean, Rebecca."

He laughs softly. "I wasn't always an old

guy," he says. "Years back I guess you would have called her my lady friend. She did rodeo; I did rodeo. We were two of a kind, at least I thought we were."

"What happened?" I asked.

"She broke her leg real bad and couldn't ride anymore. It nearly broke her heart. I offered to take care of her, but she was proud, said no charity. When Lex Stockton offered her a job, it looked like things had turned around—until I found out which job he'd offered."

"Oh Jack," I say. "How could she go from loving horses to butchering them?"

"It wasn't that simple," he says. "She thought if she took the job, she could change the way wild horses were rounded up and sold. She wanted them to gather the old and the sick for making dog food, leaving the healthy horses to live on in the wild. And for a while, she got them to listen."

"For a while?" I ask.

"They stopped listening. And I guess we stopped listening to each other, too—until last night."

"Last night when you called about Louis Blackwater?" I ask. He smiles.

"We got a start on a new understanding," he says. "Maybe that'll be my silver lining." If he's willing to give her a chance, I suppose I'll give her a chance, too.

By noon, Lex Stockton and Louis Blackwater are in police custody, and it's all over the radio and cable news. They're facing a whole list of felony charges including arson and attempted murder. Blackwater sings like a bird to avoid a lifetime in prison. He says between the divorce and a stack of bad business decisions, Stockton was facing bankruptcy. He thought cashing in on Jinx's insurance policy would save him, so he sent Blackwater to do his dirty work.

"It had to look like an accident," Jack says. "When throwing Jinx to the wolves didn't work, he ordered an inferno."

"Unbelievable," I say. "What are Peggy and her mom going to do?"

"Didn't you read Jeff's article?" he asks, shaking his head. He knows now I did not. "June Stockton filed for divorce and sold her stock in Imperial Enterprises six months before any of this went down. She's sitting on a big pile of cash and had nothing to do with her ex-husband's criminal activities. They'll manage, but Peggy is going to need a friend. You ready to take on another wild filly?"

"I'll think about it," I say, but he knows I really mean it. Peggy's lost more than I ever imagined having. I'll give her a fair chance, too.

Just then, a giant truck and trailer pulls up and interrupts Jack's treasure hunt. It's as fine as any rig I've ever seen with *Second Chance Rescue* printed on each side. A woman steps out of the driver side of the truck. Boots to hat to braided gray hair, she looks ordinary, but I see Jack smile.

"Hey, handsome," she yells. "Any of these horses need a place to stay for a while? Looks like an old cowboy burned down their barn."

"The Butcher?" I say.

"Not anymore," he smiles. "I think she's here to help rescue us all." When she walks near, he reaches out with both arms and gives her the biggest hug I've ever seen, humming that old Orleans song.

"Are you still singing that old song?" she says.

"Our song," he winks. "Now let me introduce you to my best friend, Annie, the shortest wild horse trainer I've ever known."

"Great to meet you, Annie," Rebecca says. "It's good that you're not afraid of hard work and horses. We're going to need help getting this lot loaded and settled back at my ranch."

"We're going to need a lot of help rebuilding Top Tier, too," Jack says.

"You can count on me," I tell them. "Glad to be part of the team."

"Perfect," Rebecca says. "Now let's get these glorious animals loaded."

"Let's do," I say, "and let's start with a Buckskin called Poco."

AUTHOR'S NOTE
THE FACTS BEHIND THE FICTION

The story of Annie and Poco is pure fiction, from the first word to the last. But like all stories, it had a spark of inspiration—a flicker that grew into a creative flame. The true story of fifteen-year-old Madison Wallraf provided that spark.

In April of 2012, Wallraf and her stepfather drove to the M&R Overlook Farm stable in McHenry, Illinois, and found the 25,000 square foot barn was on fire. Wallraf tossed her cell phone to her stepdad, told him to call 9-1-1, and ran into the burning building to rescue the frantic horses.

"I started off by just putting their halters on and pulling them out by twos," she told a reporter for *NBC News*. "But then the fire started getting quicker, so I just started wrapping ropes around their necks and just tying them around my arms and pulling them out."

By the time fire engines arrived, the 4'10" teenager had saved twenty-five horses from certain doom, including her own beloved pet, Red. And while she required treatment for smoke inhalation, she did make a full recovery.

The cause of the fire was unknown.

ABOUT THE AUTHOR

Kelly Milner Halls never saved a horse from a burning barn, but she did adopt a wild Mustang when she was only twelve. She and her stable master trained the fourteen-hand Buckskin named Little Bit to be a great gymkana competitor and the best friend Kelly ever had. She still has every ribbon they ever won together and the old Carpenters hit, "We've Only Just Begun," will always be their song.

Today, she lives in Spokane, Washington, with two daughters, two dogs, too many cats and a five-foot rock iguana named Gigantor. She still collects Breyer horses. Read more about Kelly and her books at www.wondersofweird.com. Email her at KellyMilnerH@aol.com.